KAREN KING

Cosmic
Whizz Kid

Illustrated by Derek Brazell

Chapter One

"Well, Shiza, we're waiting." Mr Spod fixed his beady black eyes on his pupil and twiddled his red moustache.

Shiza nervously twisted a lock of her unruly blue hair as she tried to think of an answer to the question. History wasn't her best subject. Well, actually, she didn't have a best subject. When it came to schoolwork, Shiza's brain always seemed to go to sleep.

Mr Spod coughed loudly. He was waiting for her to answer. The whole class was waiting for her to answer. She'd just have to guess. She remembered vaguely that they'd been talking about the invasion of their planet Zen by the rival planet Chang. Mr Spod probably wanted to know the year it happened.

"Er... 2047," she said, hopefully.

The class burst out laughing and Mr Spod sighed.

"Fortunately, Shiza, there were only forty-five spaceships involved in the invasion. Otherwise I don't think any of us would be here today," he said in a voice that made her feel small. "I can see you weren't paying attention to the lesson, as usual, so you can stay behind after school for an extra history lesson."

Shiza groaned. Tonight she and Meena, her best friend, were going to the Ruined City. If she stayed behind at school they wouldn't have enough time to go.

"Please sir, I can't stay behind tonight. I promised my mum I'd be straight home because we're going to the molar technician to get our teeth checked," she lied.

Mr Spod frowned. "Very well. You can do extra homework instead then."

Chapter Two

"That was quick thinking!" Meena said as
they walked out of school together and
made their way to the cosmobile park.
Everyone on Zen travelled in cosmobiles:
little brightly coloured bubble-shaped
vehicles that floated on a cushion of air
above the ground. "Not that I'd have
minded giving the Ruined City a miss.
I don't know what you find so interesting
about it."

Shiza knew Meena was scared because the Ruined City was supposed to be haunted. "Don't worry, there aren't really any ghosts," she told her. "Come on, I'll race you there!" She opened the door of her cosmobile and climbed inside. The door slid shut and a message flashed on the screen.

Shiza keyed it in and pressed another button. The cosmobile set off. The computer screen showed her that Meena was close behind. Smiling, she pressed the speed button and they both raced neck and neck, the cosmobiles always swerving or slowing down when there was any danger.

As the brightly coloured plants and trees gave way to barren dusty red ground, Shiza knew they were almost at the Ruined City. Switching on her speaker she spoke into it. "Hey, Meena, let's park the cosmoes here and take a look around."

"OK, but don't wander too far. I want to be near my cosmo if I need to make a quick getaway!" Meena replied.

Shiza chuckled. Meena was such a worrier.

They both parked their cosmobiles and got out. The air was heavy with the dust from the crumbling buildings.

"Let's take a look at the palace," Shiza said.

Meena looked horrified. "You've got to be kidding! Mr Spod said the palace could fall down at any time."

But Shiza was already making her way through the maze of ruins to the palace. Meena nervously followed her.

According to legend, the throne had magic powers and anyone who sat on it would know the answer to everything. But now only the crumbled base remained. Shiza bent down and ran her fingers over the dust. She could just make out some drawings: the sun, a half moon and a cluster of stars. As she traced their outline with her fingers, a strange feeling came over her.

"Shiza! We've got to get out of here!"
She could hear the fear in Meena's voice.
"The roof's falling in!"

A shower of dust and broken stones fell
around Shiza. She quickly stood up,
looking around in panic. Keeping her
head down, Shiza ran through the rain of
dust and falling stones to join Meena, who
was standing by the entrance.

"Come on, before it all collapses!"
Meena grabbed Shiza's arm and pulled
her back along the deserted streets.

At last they reached the safety of
their cosmobiles.

"I told you not to go into the palace.
I warned you!" Meena said angrily.
"You could have got us both killed!"

"Sorry," Shiza answered. "But just think, Meena, we were the last ones ever to look at the Zen Palace – and I even got to touch the royal throne!"

"Let's get out of here before it gets dark," Meena snapped. "I don't fancy meeting ghosts as well as almost being buried alive!"

Shiza opened the door of her cosmo and got in. Then Meena's voice came over the speaker. "Race you home, daydreamer!"

Shiza grinned, pressed the speed button and zoomed ahead of her friend. "See you there, dawddle-dog!" she shouted into the speaker.

Chapter Three

That night Shiza dreamed that she was
Queen of the Zens. She was so wise and
clever that people from every planet in the
universe came to her for advice. She was
in the middle of a meeting with all the
leaders from the other planets when her
mother shook her awake.

"Shiza, Shiza! Come on, you'll be late
for school!"

Shiza groaned and opened her eyes. If only she *was* a Queen and didn't have to go to school!

All morning she found it hard to concentrate. Her mind kept going back to yesterday's visit to the Ruined City and how strange she'd felt when she touched the throne.

"Perhaps you can answer the question for us, Shiza?" asked Mr Spod, his voice sounded mean.

Shiza stared at him blankly. What question?

"To refresh your memory, we've been talking about the Planet Noca. Perhaps you can tell us how many stars there are in the galaxy surrounding Noca?"

"1,556,789," said Shiza in a flash.

"That is correct," Mr Spod said, staring at her in amazement.

"Did you see old Spod's face when you answered that question?" giggled Meena as they walked out into the playground for break. "That sure was a lucky guess!"

"I know. It's weird but the answer just popped into my head," Shiza told her.

That afternoon the same thing happened again. Miss Popi, the art teacher, showed them an Early Zen vase

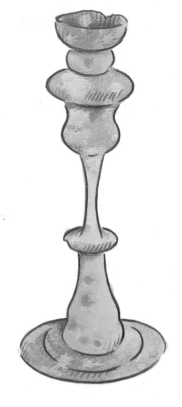

and asked if anyone knew when it was made. Shiza not only told her the date to the exact day but also who made it and where and what materials were used. There was a stunned silence, then Miss Popi beamed. "That's perfectly correct. Well done, Shiza!"

"I can't understand it. The answers just keep popping into my head," Shiza told Meena later that evening.

"It just shows that you've got a brain there somewhere," Meena teased. "You're finally remembering some of the stuff we've been taught."

Shiza frowned. "You know, I had a strange feeling when I touched the ancient Zen throne. Do you think some of the magic rubbed off and now I know everything, just like the Zen kings did?"

"Oh come on, Shi, you can't really think that crumbling piece of stone has given you magical powers?"

It did sound a bit far-fetched, Shiza had to agree. She shrugged her shoulders, "I guess you're right. Anyway, what's the big deal about getting a couple of questions right?"

Chapter Four

Shiza continued getting questions right.
Whenever anyone asked her anything the
answer just popped into her head. At first
everyone was amazed at how clever Shiza
was. They soon got used to it however,
and no one was really surprised when Mrs
Rowal, the headmistress, announced a
couple of weeks later that Shiza had been
chosen to represent the school in the
Intergalactic school quiz.

Shiza was really worried about it. "What am I going to do if the magic wears off?" she asked Meena. "I'll look a right fool and let the school down."

"For goodness sake, stop fretting about that stupid throne," Meena told her. "The truth is, now you've stopped day-dreaming you've discovered that you're really quite clever!"

Maybe she's right, Shiza thought. But deep inside her was a nagging doubt. She tried hard to swot before the quiz but nothing would stay in her mind. It was only when she was asked questions that she knew the answers.

The night before the Zen school finals Shiza was so nervous she hardly slept a wink. But she needn't have worried. She sailed through the quiz, not only answering every question but answering them so quickly that she won bonus points. There were loud cheers from her friends when the quizzmaster announced that Cosmic Grove had won the semi-finals and would represent Zen against all the other planets.

"Well done, Shiza, you've brought honour to the school," Mrs Rowal said proudly.

Shiza could hardly believe it herself. Two months ago she had been the school dunce and now she was representing the school against all the other planets. It was amazing.

Reporters soon got hold of the news and pictures of Shiza appeared in all the newspapers!

ZEN news

COSMIC WHIZZ KID wins through to final

It was all very exciting. And very worrying. For still, deep inside her, was the nagging voice telling her that it wasn't going to last. One day the magic would wear off.

Chapter Five

The finals were to be held at the Imperial Building on the planet Chang in two weeks' time. Galactic Park, the most famous school on Chang, had held the trophy for three years running and were confident they would win it again. The quiz was going to be beamed by ultra-laser to every planet in the universe so everyone could watch the contest.

Shiza woke up on the morning of the finals feeling really strange and not quite with it. "It's nerves," her mum told her. "You musn't worry. Just do your best, that's all anyone can expect."

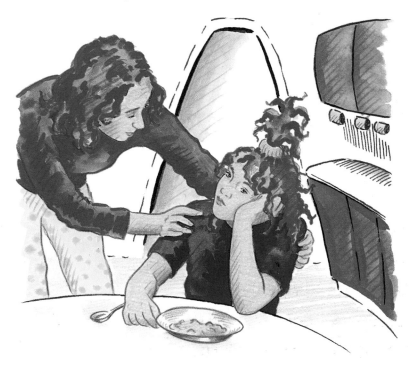

But Shiza knew that everyone expected her to win. And she wanted to win. She felt so sick and nervous that she couldn't even eat breakfast.

All too soon Mrs Rowal arrived. She was travelling with Shiza on the spaceship to Chang.

"Good luck. We're so proud of you!" Shiza's mum gave her a big hug.

Meena was waiting outside to say goodbye. "Good luck, I'll be watching you on laser-vision," she said.

Shiza gave her a weak smile. "I feel a bit strange," she said. "My head's fuzzy."

"It's nerves!" Meena told her. "You're going to be just fine."

I hope so, thought Shiza as she followed Mrs Rowal to the waiting spaceship. They sped through the universe faster than the speed of light. Stars, moons and planets flashed by until at last a bright orange glow announced that they were approaching the planet Change

As Shiza entered the Imperial Building she was greeted by loud cheers and waves from a big crowd from Zen. Shiza waved back.

"I'm famous!" Shiza thought excitedly. But when she took her seat her head felt hazy and she started to panic again.

The questions began.

How many volcanoes have erupted on the planet Thar this year?

How many moons are there in the Claco galaxy?

The answers came to her in a flash and Shiza pounced on the bell first. But when the third question came her mind went blank. It continued like this throughout the quiz, the occasional brilliant flash of knowledge followed by blankness. She was losing her power, she could feel it, although she was managing to answer enough questions to stay ahead. She only hoped she could last out until the quiz was finished.

An hour later the quiz was almost over. The only two remaining pupils were Shiza and a boy from the planet Chang. She was one question ahead.

"How many pillars are there in the intergalactical museum on the planet Noca?"

The boy from Chang hesitated.

Shiza waited for the answer to pop into her head. But it didn't. Her mind was a blank. Suddenly she knew with a sickening certainty that she'd lost the power. She was back to the old Shiza for good. And Galactic Park were going to win the trophy yet again.

"Thirty-five," the boy guessed.

"Correct," the questioner nodded. "And now for the final and deciding question. You have precisely thirty seconds to answer this, Shiza."

Shiza bit her lip anxiously.

"What was drawn on the base of the ancient Zen Kings' throne?"

Her mind was completely blank.

"You have twenty seconds left."

If only she had touched those drawings on the throne a little longer. Then the magic would have stayed a bit longer. Maybe long enough to win.

"You have ten seconds left."

Drawings? Drawings! That was it! She knew the answer!

"The sun, a half moon and a cluster of stars!" she shouted.

"That is correct," smiled the questioner.

There was a deafening round of applause. She had won! Zen had the trophy at last!

"Hooray! Three cheers for Shiza, the Cosmic Whizz Kid!"

"Well done, Shiza!"

"We've won! We've won!"

Everyone was around her, cheering her. Then she was lifted up on the crowd's shoulders and carried smiling out of the building. Zen had won!

Chapter Six

When Shiza finally returned to the spaceship with the trophy, she wondered how she was going to explain to everyone back home that she was no longer the Cosmic Whizz Kid but plain, ordinary Shiza again? Not that she minded. She'd be glad to be back to normal.

It was such a strain pretending to be something she wasn't. But it had been good to know things, so from now on she was going to stop day-dreaming, she decided, and pay attention to her lessons. Then she would know things without having to rely on magic powers.

She was so deep in thought that she didn't notice the spaceship swerve and lose control. Suddenly there was a thud and everything went dark.

"Are you all right, Shiza?"

At the sound of her mother's voice, Shiza opened her eyes. She was back at home, lying on her bed. Her mother, father and Mrs Rowal were standing over her looking worried.

"We got caught in a bad storm and had to make a bit of a crash landing," Mrs Rowal told her. "I'm afraid you had a nasty bump on the head. I hope it hasn't affected your memory."

Shiza put her hand to her forehead and sighed.

"Actually, I think it might have. My head aches and I feel a little hazy," she said. "I don't think I'm going to be able to remember things quite as well as I did before."

Then, she caught Meena's eye and winked.

Look out for more titles in the Red Storybooks series:

Mr Dunfilling and the Tasty Paste by Rob Lewis
When Mr Dunfilling invents his own toothpaste, he discovers that
when sweetener is added it can be used as rocked fuel. He builds a
rocket in the shape of a toothpaste tube and blasts off into space!
But he lands on a planet full of sugar – will events turn sour?

The Dinosaur Robbers by Jeremy Strong
Tyrannosaurus and Triceratops may look real, but they're actually
two robotic dinosaurs invented by Max's dad. However, Buster's
and Binbag's beady eyes spy the dinosaurs and decide they'll come
in handy for a spot of burglary...

Wonderwitch and the Spooks by Helen Muir
Wonderwitch and Witch Wotnot love frightening other people! So
they decide to hold a fancy dress party at Hallowe'en. Wonderwitch
will dress up as a ghost to scare the guests! But things start to go
wrong when the guests steal the witches' broomsticks...

The Tall Story by Frieda Hughes
Micky is always telling lies. Great big whopping ones. But when he
goes to stay with his grandmother by the sea, strange things keep
happening. Everything he lies about comes true...

You can buy all these books from your local bookseller, or they can
be ordered direct from the publisher. For more information about
Storybooks, write to: *The Sales Department, Macdonald Young Books,
61 Western Road, Hove, East Sussex BN3 1JD*

PRINTED IN BELGIUM BY

proost
INTERNATIONAL BOOK PRODUCTION